A Deal's a Deal!

Visit us on the Web!
www.randomhouse.com/kids

Educators and librarians, for a variety of teaching tools, visit us at
www.randomhouse.com/teachers

Library of Congress Cataloging-in-Publication Data
Blake, Stephanie.
[Donner c'est donner. English]
A deal's a deal! / written and illustrated by Stephanie Blake ;
[translated by Stephanie Blake]. — 1st American ed.
p. cm.
Summary: Simon the rabbit trades his three cars for his friend
Ferdinand's red car but when the red car breaks,
Simon tries to find a way to get his three cars back.
ISBN 978-0-375-86901-3 (trade) — ISBN 978-0-375-96901-0 (lib. bdg.)
[1. Rabbits—Fiction. 2. Toys—Fiction. 3. Play—Fiction. 4. Humorous stories.]
I. Title. II. Title: A deal is a deal!
PZ7.B565De 2011 [E]—dc22
2010021016

MANUFACTURED IN CHINA
10 9 8 7 6 5 4 3 2 1
First American Edition

A Deal's a Deal!

Written and illustrated by
Stephanie Blake

Random House 🏠 **New York**

There once was a mischievous little rabbit named Simon.

One day, Simon went over to his friend Ferdinand's to play. He brought his three cars along with him—his yellow one, his blue one, and his green one.

Simon and Ferdinand built a big racetrack.

"I'd really like to have a red car," said Simon. "Red's my favorite color."

"I have a red car. Let's trade," said Ferdinand.

"No, your car's plastic. I want a red car made of metal—it's stronger than plastic!" said Simon.

"No, it isn't. My red car is extraordinary! If you want, I'll trade it for your green one," said Ferdinand.

"It looks fake," said Simon.

"No, it doesn't. Anyhow, I don't want to trade it anymore."

"Why not?" asked Simon.

"Because it's an extraordinary car. It cost a lot, a lot more than your green car," said Ferdinand.

"Okay, okay. I'll trade all three of my cars—the yellow one, the blue one, AND the green one—for your red one," said Simon.

"Yes, but if I trade my extraordinary red car for yours, I won't have it anymore," said Ferdinand.

"But you'll have three cars instead! A yellow one, a blue one, and a green one," said Simon.

"Okay," said Ferdinand.

Simon gave his yellow car, his blue car, and his green car to Ferdinand, and Ferdinand gave his extraordinary red car to Simon.

"You can't take them back," said Ferdinand. "A deal's a deal."

"A deal's a deal," repeated Simon.

Simon walked home with his new car and showed it to his little brother.

"Ugwy," said Gaspard.

"Why?" asked Simon.

"Becuzes," answered Gaspard.

"You don't know anything—you're just a baby!" said Simon. "It's an extraordinary red car!"

But as soon as Simon started to play with his extraordinary red car—CRACK!—it broke in two.

Simon thought about the deal he'd made with Ferdinand. Had Ferdinand played a trick on him?

Suddenly he had an idea . . .
a terrible, horrible, wonderful idea!
He quickly got to work on his plan,
and when he was done, off he went
to Ferdinand's.

"Wow! My red car is really extraordinary!" said Simon. "You sure you don't want it back?"

"No way," answered Ferdinand. "A deal's a deal."

"Are you sure?" asked Simon.

"Yes!" said Ferdinand.

"Do you mean that I will never, ever have to give it back to you?"

"Never, ever," said Ferdinand.

"So I get to keep what you left in it, then," said Simon.

"Wait a minute," said Ferdinand. "I left something in it? What is it?"

"Oh, nothing. A deal's a deal!" said Simon.

"Are you crazy? If there's something in it, it's MINE!" shouted Ferdinand.

"Well, give me my yellow car, my blue car, and my green car, and I'll give you the red one back," said Simon.

Ferdinand gave back the yellow car, the blue car, and the green car.

He grabbed his red car.

"It's broken!" said Ferdinand.

He stuck a finger in it to see what sort of treasure he could possibly have left inside. . . .

It was round like a marble and all sticky and gooey. . . .

"A booger?!
Yuck!"